This book belongs to

....

www.makebelieveideas.com

Written by Rosie Greening.
Illustrated by Clare Fennell.

The Christmas SELFIE Contest

Rosie Greening • Clare Fennell

make
believe
ideas

In a big, busy workshop
with shelves full of toys,
the elves worked their socks off
and made lots of noise!

They hammered and clattered and chattered and played,

and worked as a team on the toys that they made.

But Alfie was different
from all of the rest.
He didn't like teamwork:
he liked being best!

He'd boast about all of the toys he'd create,

then show them to everyone, shouting, "I'M GREAT!"

Made by Alfie

Made by Alfie

Made by Alfie

Made by Alfie

Made by Alfie

Made by Alfie

One **morning**, the **elves**
were so **sick** of his talk,
the Head Elf said:

"Alfie, please
go for a walk!"

So Alfie went out
to the gingerbread store,
and noticed a poster
he'd not seen before...

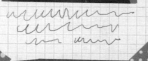

It said:

Best Selfie

Santa is holding a

SELFIE CONTEST

so send in your photos and he'll pick the best.

Young Alfie was certain he'd win it with ease.

"I'll take the best selfie –
it sounds like a breeze."

He told all his friends,
but they just got annoyed:
"There's no time for selfies –
we need to make toys!"

SANTA'S
WORKSHOP

Young Alfie ignored them and all of their fears.
He wanted to try out some selfie ideas.

He ran to the **polar bears** chilling outside.
"Please pose for a **selfie!**" he eagerly cried.

The bears made a tower and Alfie yelled, "CHEESE!"
But one of the polar bears just . . . had . . . to . . . SNEEZE!

ATCHOO!

So Alfie rushed off to a whale in the sea.

He said, "Will you pose for a selfie with me?"

But as Alfie's camera went off with a flash, the whale spurted water on him with a SPLASH!

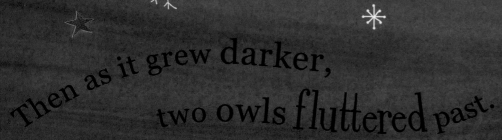

Then as it grew darker,
two owls fluttered past.

"Will you take a selfie with me?"
Alfie asked.

The group had a **hoot**,
but it still wouldn't do . . .

the sky was too **dark** . . .

and the **selfies** were too!

Poor Alfie ran back
to the workshop in tears.
"I thought I would win,
but I'm out of ideas!"

"Forget about selfies," the other elves said.
"Let's finish these toys with some teamwork instead!"

The elves got to work

and at last Alfie saw . . .

TOYS

when they worked

as a team,

they could do

so much more.

They **sanded** and **painted**

with painstaking care,

and soon there were

colorful toys **everywhere!**

"The workshop looks magical!"
young Alfie said.

And then an idea popped into his head . . .

"Let's pose for a selfie!"

he said with a grin.

I LOVE SANTA!

"With all of us in it, this selfie could win!"

He sent off the **selfie** and to his **surprise**,

he got a reply saying:

You've won first prize!

1st

I LOVE
SANTA!

Your prize is a sleigh ride

with Santa himself.

Congrats on your selfie –

you're one lucky elf!

Young Alfie was thrilled,

and he knew what to do.

He showed all his friends

and said, "You should come too!"

When Santa arrived in his beautiful sleigh,
the elves clambered in, then they went on their way.

And as Santa's reindeer soared into the skies,
young Alfie was glad they had all shared his prize!

THE END